AF496643

# The Gran Bwa Forest

Written by R. Kwinn

Illustrated by Dan Ruja

atmosphere press

© 2024 R. Kwinn

Published by Atmosphere Press

No part of this book may be reproduced without permission from the author except in brief quotations and in reviews. This is a work of fiction, and any resemblance to real places, persons, or events is entirely coincidental.

atmospherepress.com

For the dreamers, the lovers of nature, the wild child with wind in her hair and mischief in her eyes, the valiant tree huggers, the beachgoers and day trippers, sophisticated city slickers and gallant earth explorers, sun worshipers and night chasers, this breath of fresh air is for you. Inspired by the natural elegance of this magical place that we all call home.

She walked along the budding path, deep within the woodlands, deep within her own mind - not thinking of herself or of what time it may be, as she was in awe of this very moment. The majestic surroundings cast a spell of sorts, leaving the celestial creature wide-eyed and wondering what secrets might be kept in this serene world all around.

A harmonious hum blissfully buzzed as the music of the forest sent her along with a giddy hop to each light step taken into the great unknown.

Down the trail she floated, stopping to carefully kneel and caress a cluster of vibrant little mushrooms that had caught her attention. Sweet hues of earthy, velvet mauve and crinkly pure white pulled her in, startling her as sleepy eyes opened, and delicate, childlike arms reached out.

Playfully, they grabbed and giggled at her innocent and jovial expense, whilst their tiny hands tickled her fingertips as they held on, balancing and pulling themselves up. The ground was brimming with gleeful chatter as their webbed feet met the soft grass below—colorful and lively, it filled her with absolute delight.

She watched as they let go and joined together, creating a circle that illuminated the morning mist.

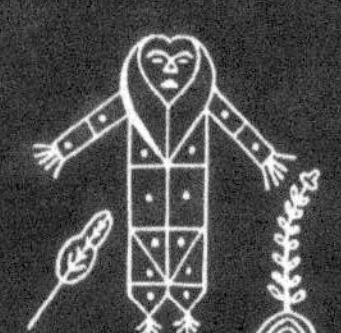

A movement in the brush ahead distracted her focus.
Upon looking up, she witnessed what could possibly
be the greatest beauty in all the land.

Gazing back, she hoped for one more chance to
connect, only to meet with a leafy blanket abound
with twinkling sparkles floating in the early
sunlight—the underwood beings, gone.

She humbly approached this immense fellow, feeling a strength, a pull, a radiating energy she had never felt before—welcoming, powerful, all-knowing. His willowy branches extended to the highest points of the wooded haven, stretching to reach the vast embrace of the infinite skies above.

The grand ancient was draped in the deepest and richest shades of emerald green, embodying the watchful spirit and the very essence of life itself. Providing solace below his furthest spread, his dark bark was thick and wrinkled, weathered but not worn, with roots firmly anchored beneath the sandy creekbed below. He lightly touched the others surrounding him, and they bowed in appreciation of his stoic grace.

She wondered what was locked up inside of this divine guardian, stories to be told, had she the ability to understand the language within.

A gust suddenly arose, caressing her curiosities with mysterious truths, whirling them into a tornado adorned with petals and leaves. This realm, guarded by the protector, was softly speaking, voices echoing o'er and about in rhythm with the ebb and flow of life below.

The flowers, the fern, the fir, the wilderness seemed to be calling, perhaps beckoning, only to her in these seconds of sweet solitude, and here she found herself captivated. She knew the endless existence of this world was always close, unruly, and free, adventurous and unbound.

Radiance glistened and bounced, skipping over the rocks and through the tall reeds and grasses. Every last bit of the rippled bank was decorated with delicate, dewy webs and hundreds, possibly thousands, of demure blossoms and buds, holding on with all of their might.

Pure bliss it was.

An excited shiver ran up her spine as her attention
was drawn towards a lively group, their opalescent
tailfins splashing in the dayglow. Venturing, they
dove and brought up treasures of the underworld,
decorating themselves with shells and pearls,
clams and lustrous gems.

A fair-skinned figure departed, a mesmerizing tune escaping her lips as she effortlessly glided towards the shallows. Entranced by both movement and sound, the ethereal obeyed the call of the song and splashed into the water without hesitation, surrendering to the irresistible pull. As she submerged, her flesh prickled with cold, an unexpected sense of calm washing over her. Descending unwillingly, she watched as refractions of light from above shone down upon her.

It was quiet. She was numb. The last few air bubbles escaped her mouth, and she didn't seem to mind as the colors began to fade. Darkness weaved in and out as revelations of the untold approached. She would finally know what was not.

A sudden burst of laughter pierced the veil of calm, and as quickly as she was lured in, she was pulled back into the moment. She hastily surfaced, breaking through the water, gasping for air. Relief flooded her as she found herself close to shore, safe from the eerie depths below. She emerged unscathed, relieved, and safe near the treeline.

As she composed her thoughts and dried off, the siren who had cast the spell moved close once again. Carefully, she removed something from her neck and handed her a charmed amulet—the symbolic rite of passage.

With a sigh of lighthearted relief,
the gift was accepted.

Gazing down at the wondrous piece, she absorbed
each facet of the glowing crystal, marveling and
reveling at what had happened. She wanted to
ask, only to find the choir gone, carrying on and
playing elsewhere, her kindred nowhere
to be seen.

A slight breeze snagged her arm as she turned to move on and away. Extending her slender, elegant hands, she could feel it playfully tousle her long, golden mane, pulling on the new treasure nestled against her neck.

A dream it was, levitating under the daytime clouds, drifting through this place full of untamed delight and violet moments.

A rustle in the not-so-far distance moved
the calm scene across from her.

There, on the lush grassy knoll, stood a brilliant
snow-colored wolf, his intense amber gaze sizing
her up. His fur shimmered as if he had just risen
from the  silvery and welcoming rift below. His
magnetic presence held the color of curiosity,
a shade unreserved.

Somehow, he reached out and touched her
deeply and as they both stood frozen, he could
see into her heart, and she, into his wild soul.

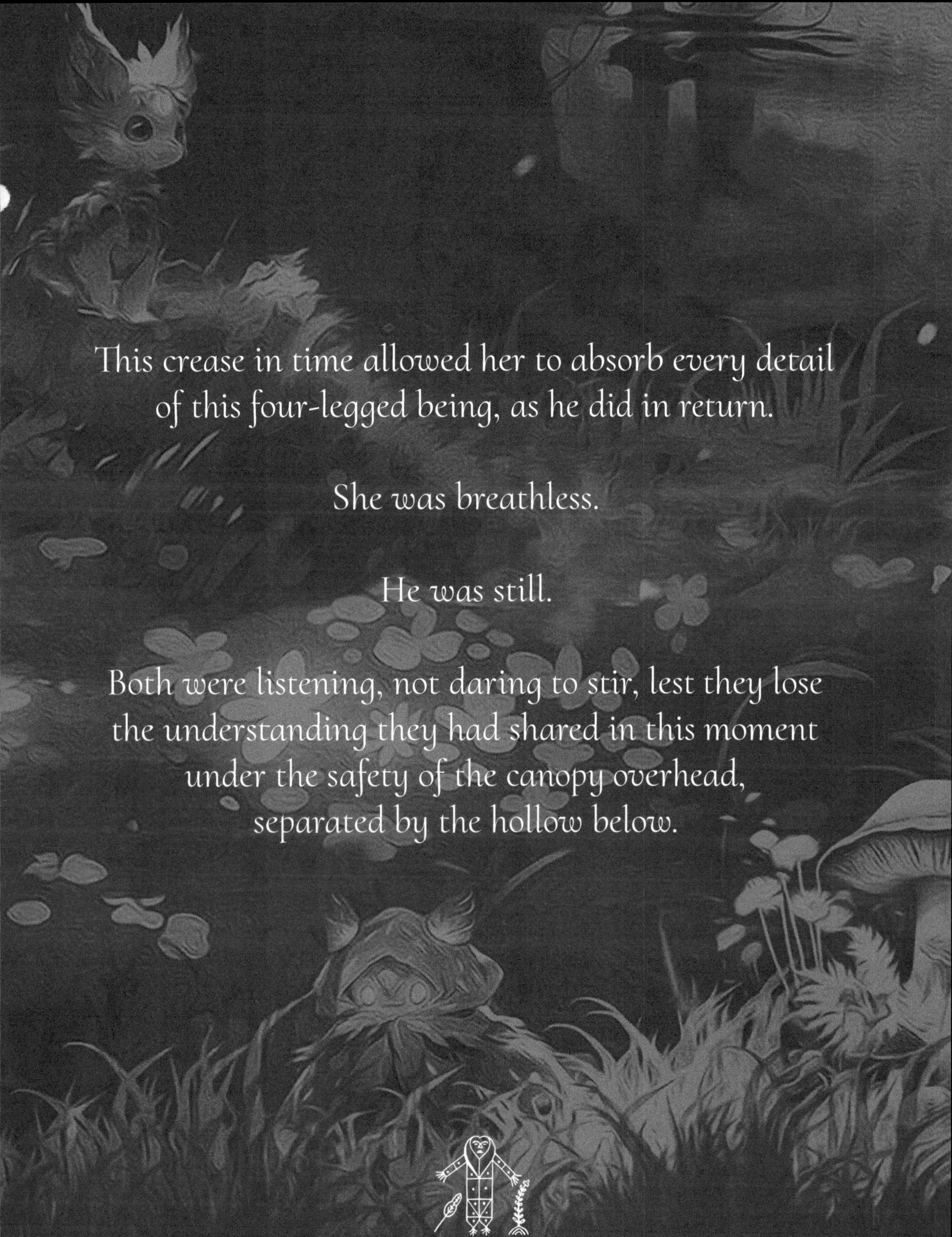

This crease in time allowed her to absorb every detail
of this four-legged being, as he did in return.


She was breathless.


He was still.


Both were listening, not daring to stir, lest they lose
the understanding they had shared in this moment
under the safety of the canopy overhead,
separated by the hollow below.

The shrill cry of the night hawk rang true above.

Her fierce and spirited call echoed over the hills,
signaling the return of the evening, conjuring the
watcher, disrupting the enamored silence, filling
the air with anticipation.

Looking away, they both faded back into the
rhythmic sway, the chirr of the katydid, and
the dance of the fae. With a glance over his
sleek, fleecy shoulder, the mighty beast turned
and slowly padded away, continuing his
journey into the humming grove.

Where he may roam, she may never chance
upon, yet she was at peace in the uncertainty.
This fleeting encounter would forever be
cherished, as would her connection
with this glorious land.

Inhaling every luminous hue, the nymph filled
her lungs with an unparalleled sense
of fulfillment.

Carefully, she followed the trail one thousand
woodland creatures traversed before her - and
most certainly would after - unsure of where it
would lead, unsure of what may lie ahead.

With wanderlust whispering, she smiled and
pushed on, the fading warmth on her skin
and the adventure in her heart.


This was her path, her life.


This was her story.

# About the Author

Kwinn traversed the globe in solitude,
Echoed screams seeping into vast darkness,
Unearthed wild magick in depths of silence,
Foraged the macabre and sparkling,
Aligning herself with a barefoot gremlin,
Together, boldly venturing into the uncharted,
Questing for fortune,
Searching for fame,
Weaving tales of shadow and light,
These creatures of legend persist in their journey,
Into and through the great unknown.

# About the Illustrator

Dan Ruja is an illustrator living in Bucharest, Romania. He has a Bachelor's degree in Arts and graphic design. In 2014, he found that painting is the best way to relax and since then he has painted very often. Art is the bond between himself and the child within him that he doesn't want to give up in exchange for adulthood.

# About Atmosphere Press

Atmosphere Press is an independent, full-service publisher for excellent books in all genres and for all audiences. Learn more about what we do at atmospherepress.com.

We encourage you to check out some of Atmosphere's latest releases, which are available at Amazon.com and via order from your local bookstore:

*Melody in Exile*, by S.T. Grant
*Covenant*, by Kate Carter
*Near Scattered Praise Lies Our Substantial Endeavor*,
    by Ron Penoyer
*Weightless, Woven Words*, by Umar Siddiqui
*Journeying: Flying, Family, Foraging*, by Nicholas Ranson
*Lexicon of the Body*, by DM Wallace
*Controlling Chaos*, by Michael Estabrook
*Almost a Memoir*, by M.C. Rydel
*Throwing the Bones*, by Caitlin Jackson
*Like Fire and Ice*, by Eli
*Sway*, by Tricia Johnson

*A Patient Hunger*, by Skip Renker
*The Carcass Undressed*, by Linda Eguiliz
*Poems That Wrote Me*, by Karissa Whitson
*Gnostic Triptych*, by Elder Gideon
*For the Moment*, by Charnjit Gill